BULLY "ME" NOT, PLEASE

Shirley Patterson

To order additional copies of this book, contact:
Xlibris
844-714-8691
www.Xlibris.com
Orders@Xlibris.com

ISBN: Softcover   978-1-6641-1906-2
         EBook   978-1-6641-1932-1

Print information available on the last page.

Rev. date: 10/02/2020

About the Author

Shirley Patterson was born in Woodbine Georgia and is a devoted mother of 15 children. She has been a role model grandmother to 23 grandchildren, 1 great grandchild and another great grandchild due October 2020. Growing up she developed a love for many sports and participated in them extensively. Shirley was heavily involved in the community. Her passion for people is expressed through her poetry, short stories, songs and writings about life. Her love for people was consistently on display through pastoring of a church, directing praise teams, youth and adult choirs. In Shirley's journey of life she experienced bullying first hand on all levels as a child, in adulthood, with her children and family. Unfortunately, bullying has no boundaries and crosses many lines. Even as a black woman she still feels the effects of bullying. Shirley's passion to shed light on bullying has been transformed into a little story, which was inspired by her own experiences. She not only witnessed bullying but was a victim herself. Through faith and courage her perspective changed from victim to **Victor**! Within her pain, she **Perfected** her praise and discovered the mystery to this thing called *bullying*.

In a very small place, there was this little ant named Will. He was smaller and a little different than the other ants. Every day of his life was always a test.

In that same small place, there was Big Ant who harassed Will every day. Big Ant thought making fun of the little ant was okay.

One day, while Will was walking home, he heard a sound, as if someone were crying. He was not used to hearing Big Ant cry. Will was alone so he tipped quietly to see what was wrong. To his great surprise, there was Big Ant who always harassed and bullied him.

Big Ant was crying with heavy tears in his eyes and talking to himself as if someone else was there with him. "Why day after day when all I want to do is go out and play?" He sighed heavily, "I am beaten and mistreated all day long!" Big Ant was being beat and made to cry, thinking to himself, "what have I done?" "Please somebody, can you tell me why?"

Will tried to get closer to hear what was going on but slipped and almost fell.

When Big Ant turned around, he was very surprised to see Will. Tears were streaming down his face as he suddenly rushed towards Will who was so afraid.

Big Ant in his haste tripped over a limb, fell and bumped his head. This bully now lay shaking, afraid, and crying out, "help me please," while holding his head.

Will ran to help him up, but did not know what Big Ant would do. Will was always taught when someone needs help, help is what we must do.

At that moment, Will realized hurting ants or hurting people, hurt other ants and other people too. They are those who are experiencing hurt themselves. It was the same thing the big ant was doing to Will.

When Big Ant stood on his feet Will was shaking mightily. He could barely speak. Then Will heard him say in a very low voice, "you could have left me here."

To this Will replied, "I only had one choice, because we are helpers one to another." "It does not matter if you are not like me, the size of me, or the same color as me, you are still my brother."

To my loving supporters

My 15 children who always "got my back!"

Jay and Jacob, my boys !

Bryant and Nesie Walker - Bryant's Cooling and Heating - Kingsland, GA. Pastor Bobby

Donaldson - It's All About Jesus Outreach Ministries, Inc. - Greenwood, FL.

Jessica Williams - Outstanding Sponsor - Folkston, GA.

Deacon Jerry and Linda Gail Monlyn - Blountstown, FL.

Pastor Chuckie and Anna Freeman - Christ Church - Daytona, FL.

Deacon Kelosky Chambers - Blountstown, FL.

Chris Garrett - Blountstown, FL.

Veronica Sullivan - Kingsland, GA.

Maacha Cheesmon - Blountstown, FL.

Ian Donaldson - Marianna, FL.

Pastor & First Lady Vanessa Dubois - Zarephath Victory Tabernacle - Kingsland, GA.

Anna, Kisha, Squeaky - thank you for the flyers and background work

Last but not least, my CD creator, recorder and musician Joshua Patterson of JP Recordings

CPSIA information can be obtained
at www.ICGtesting.com
Printed in the USA
BVHW022325050121
597069BV00002B/19